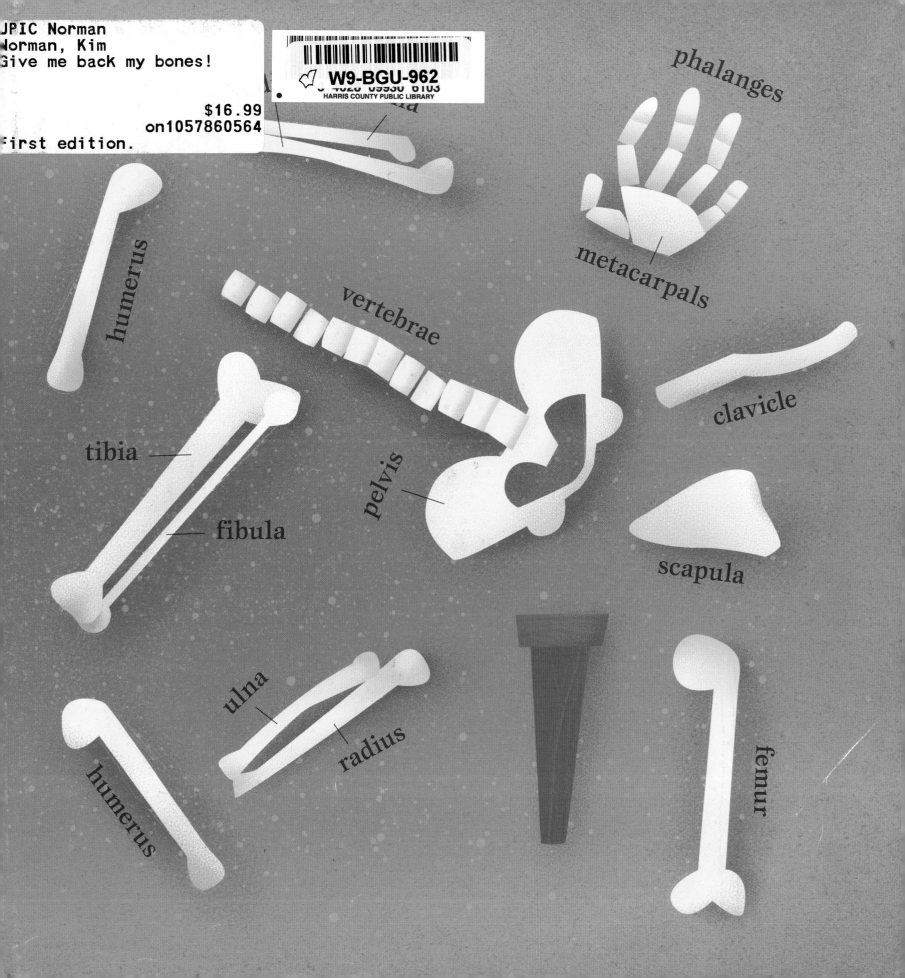

phalanges

metacarpals

humerus

vertebrae

clavicle

tibia

fibula

pelvis

scapula

ulna

radius

humerus

femur

GIVE ME BACK MY BONES!

KIM NORMAN

illustrated by BOB KOLAR

CANDLEWICK PRESS

A stormy night has passed here
and toppled every mast here.
The ocean, flowing fast here,
has scattered all my bones!

Help me find my head bone,
my pillowed-on-the-bed bone,
the pirate's flag-of-dread bone —
I'm scouting out my skull.

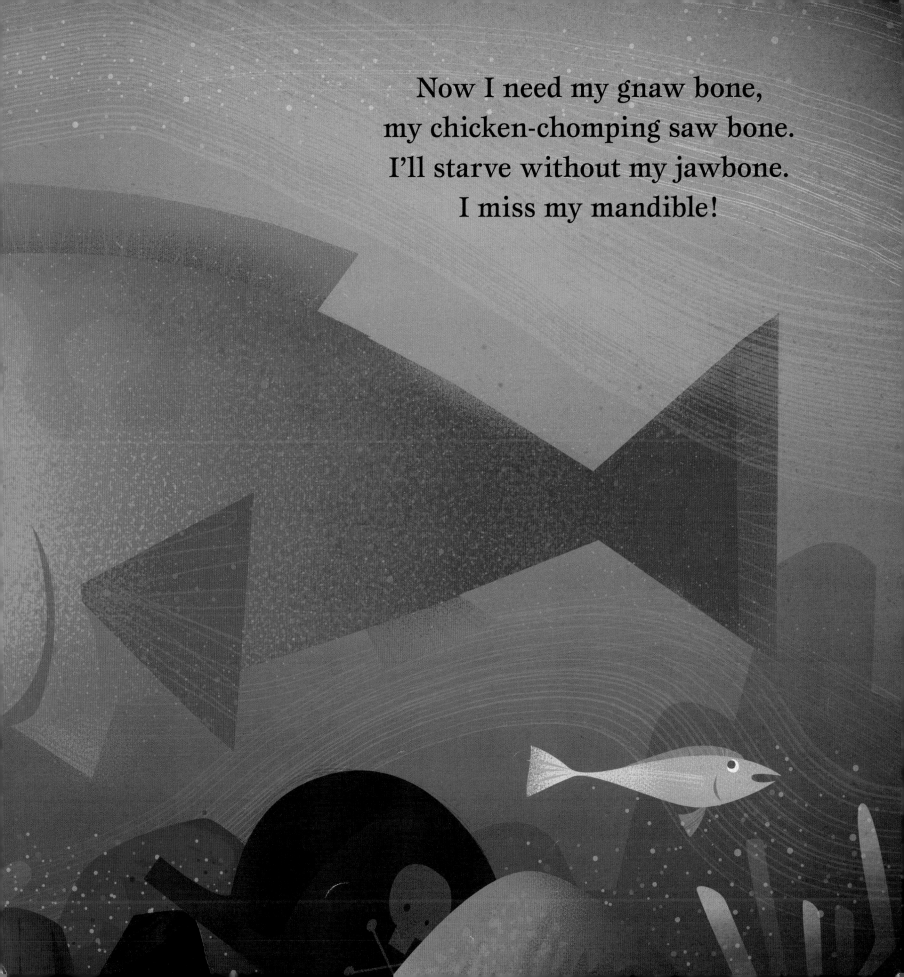

Now I need my gnaw bone,
my chicken-chomping saw bone.
I'll starve without my jawbone.
I miss my mandible!

Collar me a collarbone,
the way-down-where-I-swaller bone,
a handy parrot-hauler bone —
I claim my clavicle.

Give me back my breastbone,
the center-of-my-chest bone,
the hold-my-ribs-the-best bone —
return my sturdy sternum.

Who can spot my shoulder blade,
my shrugging jacket-holder blade,
my shiver-when-I'm-colder blade?
Oh, scapula, come back!

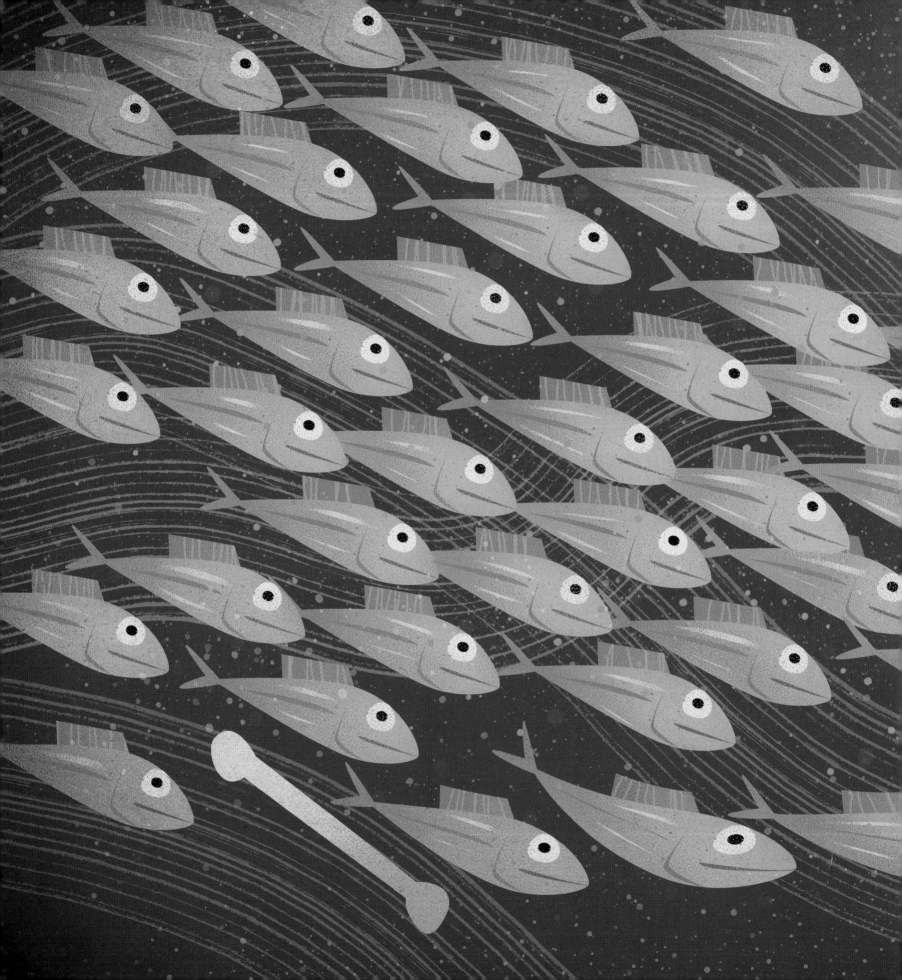

Find my upper arm bone,
the shield-my-face-from-harm bone,
that armpit-of-alarm bone—
I hanker for my humerus.

Don't forget my forearms,
those twisty, wristy chore arms.
I'll jingle-jangle more charms
on radius and ulna.

I'm grasping for some hand bones,
my wave-ahoy-to-land bones
or dig-a-hole-in-sand bones —
I miss my metacarpals.

And still I lack my back bones,
my haul-a-heavy-sack bones,
my strung-up-in-a-stack bones—
return my vertebrae.

Next I need two thighbones,
those top-of-leggy high bones,
my strapping, slapping spry bones.
Has someone seen my femurs?

I'm sunk without my swim pins,
my peg-leg-popping slim pins,
those gangplank-walking shin twins—
called tibia and fibula.

Tickle out my toe bones,
the piggies-in-a-row bones,
my leather-booted low bones —
I miss my fair phalanges.

At last! I've got my lost bones,
no longer skull-and-crossed bones,
my milky ocean-tossed bones . . .
Avast! I need . . .

a ship!

Now, cast a spyglass 'round here
while breakers curl and pound here.
There's treasure to be found here—
I feel it in my bones!

For Skylar and Nina,
who know lots of big science words
K. N.

For Olivia, who helps put lots
of bones back where they belong
B. K.

First edition 2019

Library of Congress Catalog Card Number pending
ISBN 978-0-7636-8841-7

19 20 21 22 23 24 APS 10 9 8 7 6 5 4 3 2 1

Printed in Humen, Dongguan, China

This book was typeset in Esprit Medium.
The illustrations were created digitally.

Candlewick Press
99 Dover Street
Somerville, Massachusetts 02144

visit us at www.candlewick.com

metacarpals

radius

ulna

humerus

scapula

sternum

skull

mandible

clavicle

clavicle

scapula

humerus